D1099055

big & SMALL

Original Korean text by Cecil Kim
Illustrations by Mique Moriuchi
Original Korean edition © Yeowon Media Co., Ltd. 2009

This English edition published by Big & Small in 2014
by arrangement with Yeowon Media Co., Ltd.
English text edited by Joy Cowley
English edition © Big & Small 2014

ISBN: 978-1-921790-76-8

Printed in Korea

The Three Bears

Written by Cecil Kim Illustrated by Mique Moriuchi
Edited by Joy Cowley

Three bears live in a house.
Biggest Bear is the biggest.
Big Bear is smaller.
Little Bear is the smallest.

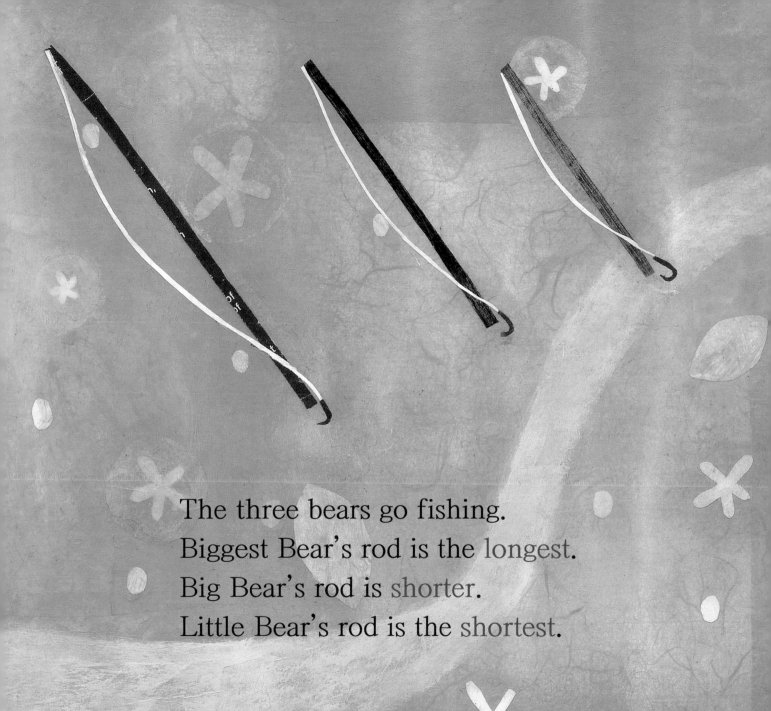

The three bears go fishing.
Biggest Bear's rod is the longest.
Big Bear's rod is shorter.
Little Bear's rod is the shortest.

The bears wait for the fish.
They wait and wait and wait.

Whip!

They get some fish!
Biggest Bear's fish is the biggest.
Big Bear's fish is smaller.
Little Bear's fish is the smallest.

The three bears put on their hats.
Biggest Bear's hat is the biggest.
Big Bear's hat is smaller.
Little Bear's hat is the smallest.

Tug!

They pull carrots
from the garden.

Biggest Bear's carrot is the biggest.
Big Bear's carrot is smaller.
Little Bear's carrot is the smallest.

The Bears go out for water.
Biggest Bear's bucket is the biggest.
Big Bear's bucket is smaller.
Little Bear's bucket is the smallest.

Splash!

They get water from the well.

10

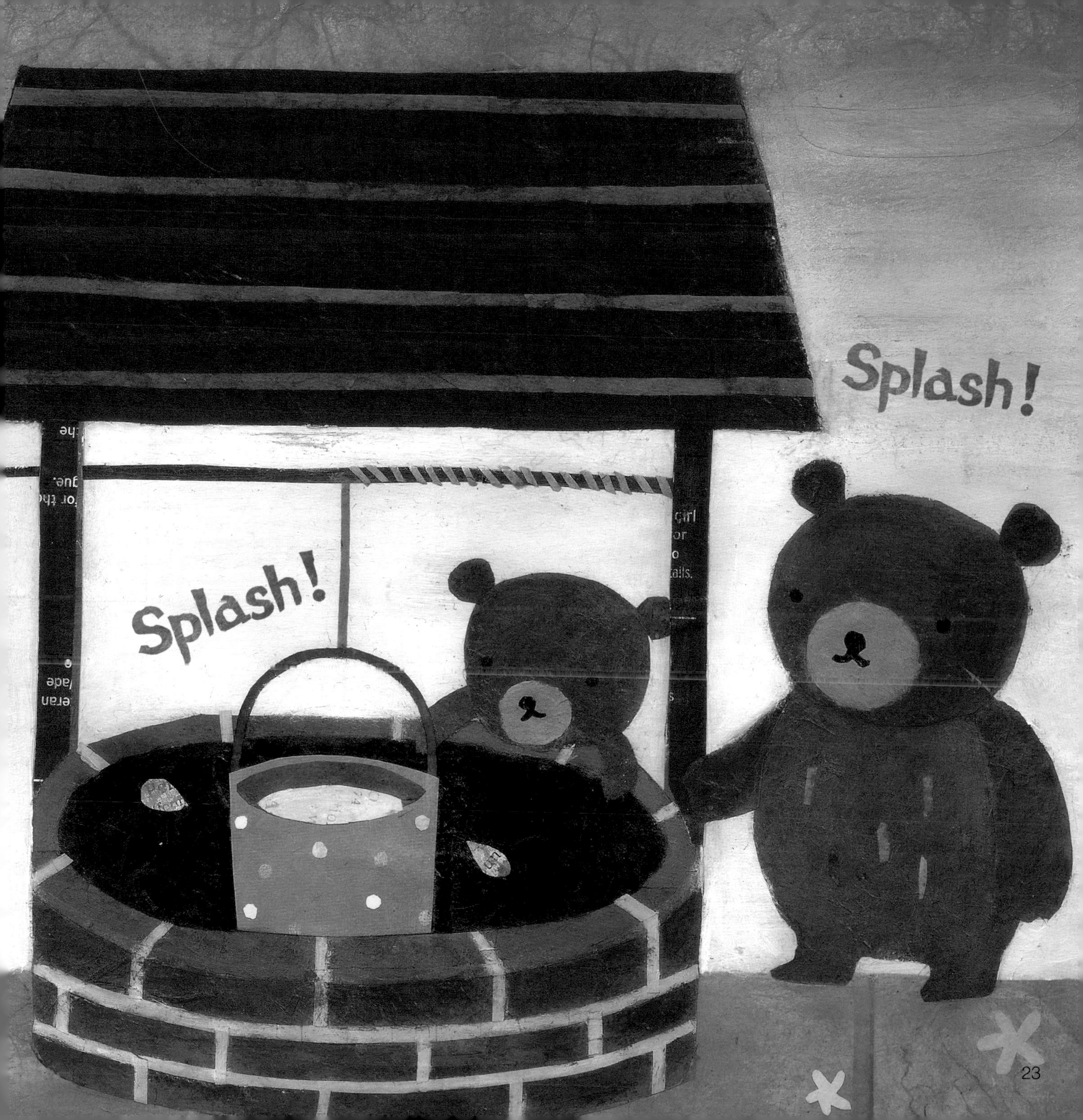
Splash!
Splash!

The water
and the carrots
and the fish
go in the pot.

The bears are
making soup.

Who will have the biggest bowl?

Little Bear has the biggest bowl!
He will grow big and strong!